I Can Do It Myself!

For Emily, Tyler, and Jocelyn
And for my very capable nieces and nephews: Adam, Andrew, Billy, Blake, Caroline,
Connor, Danielle, Ellie, Isaac, Joel, Justin, Kathleen, Lisa, and Luke—D. A.

For Brian & Liz and David & Amy—N. H.

Published by
PEACHTREE PUBLISHERS
1700 Chattahoochee Avenue
Atlanta, Georgia 30318-2112
www.peachtree-online.com

Text © 2009 by Diane Adams
Illustrations © 2009 by Nancy Hayashi

First trade paperback edition published in 2013

Book design by Nancy Hayashi
Cover design by Loraine Joyner
Composition by Melanie McMahon Ives

Illustrations created in watercolor, pen, and colored pencil. Text typeset in Baskerville
Infant; title typeset in Apple's Chalkboard.

Printed in November 2017 by Imago in Singapore
10 9 8 7 6 5 4 (hardcover)
10 9 8 7 6 5 4 (trade paperback)

HC: 978-1-56145-471-6
PB: 978-1-56145-725-0

Library of Congress Cataloging-in-Publication Data

Adams, Diane, 1960-
  I can do it myself! / written by Diane Adams ; illustrated by Nancy Hayashi. — 1st ed.
    p. cm.
  Summary: Emily Pearl is a big girl who insists on doing everything for herself until
evening, when having someone help her get ready for bed is nice.
  [1. Self-reliance—Fiction. 2. Bedtime—Fiction.] I. Hayashi, Nancy, ill. II. Title.
PZ8.3.A213Iaac 2009
  [E]—dc22
                                    2008031117

I Can Do It Myself!

Written by Diane Adams
Illustrated by Nancy Hayashi

PEACHTREE
ATLANTA

Emily Pearl is a very big girl.

She can pour her own juice.

She can tie her own shoes.

She can feed her cat Fred,
and her goldfish Ted, too.

And if just for one second her mom tries to help,
Emily says, "I can do it myself!"

She can make her own bed,

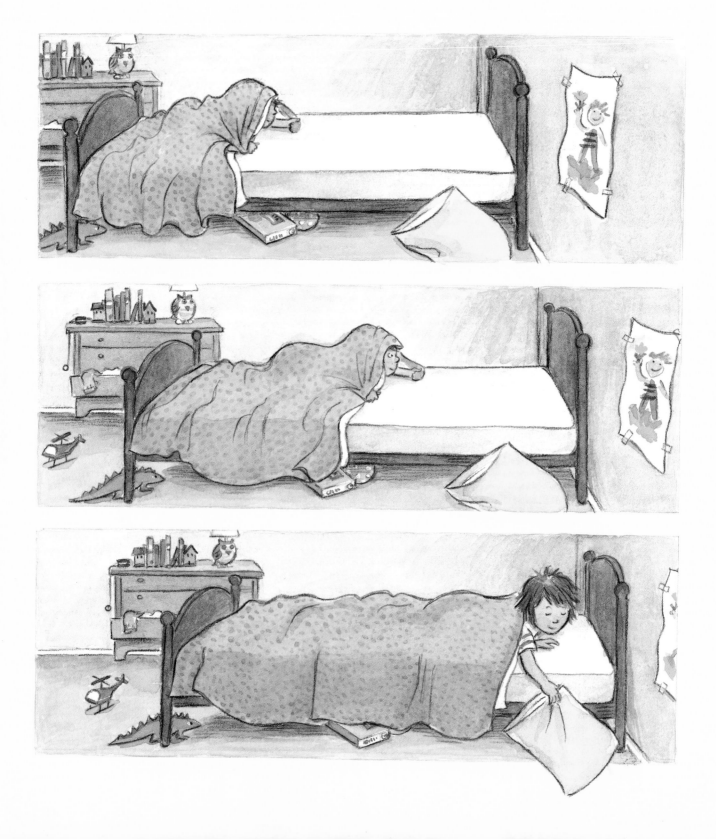

peanut butter her bread,

and play the trombone while she stands on her head.

And if just for one second her mom tries to help,
Emily says, "I can do it myself!"

She can brush her own teeth.

She can curl her own hair.

She can paint her own pictures
of rabbits and bears.

And if just for one second
her mom tries to help,
Emily says, "I can do it myself!"

Emily Pearl is
a very big girl.

She can fold her own clothes.
She can clean her own room.

She can sweep up her crumbs
with the long-handled broom.

And if just for one second her
mom tries to help,
Emily says, "I can do it myself!"

She can wash her own face.

She can blow her own nose.

She can scrub herself clean
from her head to her toes.

And if just for one second her mom tries to help,
Emily says, "I can do it myself!"

But at bedtime when shadows creep over the wall,
Emily Pearl feels a teeny bit small.

"Will you read me a story,

and hug me real tight?

Will you find my bear Binkie,
and keep on the light?"

Now Emily knows she can do this herself,
but sometimes it's nice...

...to let someone else.